The Copycat

Kathleen and Donald Hersom
illustrated by Catherine Stock

ATHENEUM   1989   NEW YORK

I have a cat, a bold copycat,
who lurks in the cow shed
to moo at the cow,

And sprawls in the pigsty
and grunts at the sow.

I have a cat, a bold copycat,
who floats on the duck pond
and quacks at the drakes,

And slides through the heather
to hiss at the snakes.

I have a cat, a bold copycat,
who sleeps in a kennel
and barks at the dog,

And jumps in the water
to croak at the frog.

I have a cat, a bold copycat,
who flits to and fro
in the dusk with the bats,

And scuttles and squeaks
in the barn with the rats.

I have a cat, a bold copycat, who clucks in the farmyard and pecks at the fowls,

And startles the graveyard,
outscreeching the owls.

I have a cat, a bold copycat,
who trots to the stable
and neighs at the mare,

Who leaps up the hillside
to dance with the hare,

And copycats me
when I cuddle my bear!

Do you have a cat,
a stay-at-home cat,
who would sit
on a mat…

And teach
Meow!
to my cat?

To Natalie, Timothy,
Steadman, Wendy, Matthew, Herman,
Ellen, and Tony, with love—K.H. and D.H.

For Elaine—C.S.

Atheneum
Macmillan Publishing Company
866 Third Avenue, New York, NY 10022
Collier Macmillan Canada, Inc.
First Edition
Printed in Hong Kong by South China Printing Co.

10 9 8 7 6 5 4 3 2 1

Library of Congress Cataloging-in-Publication Data
Hersom, Kathleen
The copycat/by Kathleen and Donald Hersom;
illustrations, Catherine Stock.   p. cm.
Summary: A story in verse about a cat who enjoys imitating the sounds of other animals.
ISBN 0-689-31448-5
[1. Cats—Fiction. 2. Animal sounds—Fiction. 3. Stories in rhyme.]
I. Hersom, Donald. II. Stock, Catherine, ill. III. Title.
PZ8.3.H437Co 1989 [E]—dc19 88-34166 CIP AC